How can you lose
a mammoth tusk?

Penny and Ms. Siscoe heard a scream coming from the exhibit area.

"What's that?" asked Ms. Siscoe.

"It's Brian!" shouted Penny. "I'd know that scream anywhere."

Penny ran to their display.

"It's missing!" Brian shouted, pointing at the exhibit. "Somebody took our tusk! Somebody wanted to ruin our science project!"

Penny's mouth dropped open. Brian was right. The mammoth tusk had disappeared!

Also by Elizabeth Levy

A Mammoth Mix-Up

Starring
Brian and Pea Brain

by Elizabeth Levy
illustrated by George Ulrich

HarperTrophy
A Division of HarperCollinsPublishers

To the real Nancy Siscoe,
Katherine Brown Tegen, and Tyler—
true mystery companions of Brian, Penny, and me

A MAMMOTH MIX-UP
Starring Brian and Pea Brain
Text copyright © 1995 by Elizabeth Levy
Illustrations copyright © 1995 by George Ulrich

Library of Congress Cataloging-in-Publication Data
Levy, Elizabeth.
   A mammoth mix-up : Starring Brian and Pea Brain / by Elizabeth
Levy ; illustrated by George Ulrich.
      p.   cm.
   Summary: Brian and his younger sister Penny become involved in a
mystery at the science museum where they are working on a woolly
mammoth display for a science fair.
   ISBN 0-06-024814-9. — ISBN 0-06-024815-7 (lib. bdg.)
   ISBN 0-06-442043-4 (pbk.)
   [1. Science projects—Fiction.   2. Brothers and sisters—Fiction.
3. Mystery and detective stories.]   I. Ulrich, George, ill.   II. Title.
PZ7.L5827Mam   1995   94-47960
[Fic]—dc20   CIP
                                                                                   AC

❖
First Harper Trophy edition, 1996.

CONTENTS

MY SISTER IS SINKING

"I'm bored," said Penny. It had been raining for days. A bored Penny was a dangerous Penny. That's when she usually thought up ways to bother her brother, Brian. Brian was in no mood to be pestered. He needed an idea for the science fair at the science museum. So far all of his ideas seemed dull.

Penny watched a fat raindrop hit the window. "I've got it. The rain forest! We could do our project on that."

Brian rolled his eyes. "I'm sick of rain, even in the forest. Besides, Pea Brain, they do the rain forest in kindergarten."

Penny made a face. After all, she *was* in

1

kindergarten. And she didn't exactly love the nickname Pea Brain. Brian called her that whenever he was annoyed with her, which was most of the time.

"How about dinosaurs?" suggested Penny.

Brian sighed. "Dinosaurs have been done to death, Pea Brain."

"Stop calling me Pea Brain," said Penny.

"Stop being one," said Brian. "Leave me alone. I really want to think of something good. All great scientists work alone."

Penny threw her stuffed dinosaur at her brother.

"Cut it out!" yelled Brian. "Geesh! I bet Einstein didn't have to deal with a little sister."

"What kind of jokes did Einstein make?" asked Penny.

"I don't know and I don't care," said Brian.

"Wisecracks," said Penny, laughing at her own joke. She had gotten it from a book that her Uncle Mike had given her. Uncle Mike was famous for his love of good food and bad jokes.

"Will you get out of here?" Brian groaned.

"Why don't you go outside?"

"It's muddy out there," said Penny, staring out the window.

"Good. Maybe the earth will swallow you whole."

"That's not nice," said Penny.

Brian stared at his computer screen. He tapped in some words.

"Okay, I'm leaving. But you'll miss me when I'm gone," warned Penny.

"I'll chance it," said Brian.

Penny stuck out her tongue at him. She wandered into the kitchen and opened the refrigerator.

"Are you hungry?" asked Penny's mother, who was doing some work at the kitchen table.

Penny shook her head. "I'm just browsing," she said. She shut the refrigerator door and sighed. "I'm terminally bored. And Brian's being a pain. Of course, he's always a pain in the neck."

"Penny," warned Mrs. Casanova. "That's not a nice way to talk about your brother."

"I'm just being honest," said Penny.

"There's such a thing as being too honest for your own good."

Penny wasn't sure that her mother was right. After all, Brian *was* a pain. She went to the back hall and put on her slicker and her boots.

"It's raining cats and dogs," her mother warned.

"At least it's not raining Brian brains. I'm going steer crazy."

"I think you mean stir crazy. Maybe some fresh air will do you good. But be careful when you open the door. Don't let Flea out." Flea was the Casanovas' orange cat, which Mrs. Casanova had found at a flea market.

But Flea had been waiting for her chance to escape all day, and when Penny opened the door, the cat scooted out.

"Whoops," said Penny, putting her hand to her mouth. "Don't worry," she shouted, "I'll get her. It'll give me something to do." She ran out into their backyard.

Brian looked out the window. He could see

Penny's yellow slicker as she chased Flea around the plum tree. Brian laughed when Penny slipped in the mud, practically doing a split. One rubber boot went around one side of the tree trunk—the other skidded around the other. Penny landed on her rump. Flea jumped on top of her.

Then something amazing happened. Penny began to sink. It was as if the ground around the tree had turned into a blobby mouth of mud.

Brian opened the window to see better. He couldn't believe it. His sister was sinking. It was a little like a dream come true. The earth was swallowing her whole.

SHARE IS NOT MY FAVORITE WORD

"Help!" shouted Penny. Brian hesitated a second. Then he saw Penny's face looking up at him. She looked really scared.

"I'm coming!" he shouted.

Brian ran out the back door into the rain. He jumped into the mud hole. Mud squished up over his sneakers. Penny was in it up to her waist. Flea had jumped out of the mud onto a branch and was safely looking down at them.

Brian struggled to push Penny to the edge of the hole. It was now almost three feet around and about two feet deep. Mud covered Penny to her chin.

Mr. and Mrs. Casanova came running out.

"What happened?" asked Mr. Casanova. "Are you both okay?"

"Penny fell into a mud hole," said Brian. "And I jumped in to save her."

"You said you wanted the earth to swallow me," said Penny. Brian looked guilty. "But you *did* come to save me," she admitted quickly.

"All this rain must have caused a sinkhole," said Mrs. Casanova. "Give me your hands, Penny, and I'll pull you out."

"Something's poking me," she complained as her mother pulled her free. Penny was covered in mud. She reached up and grabbed Flea out of the tree. Flea looked mad. Cats hate to get muddy. Penny didn't mind at all. She thought it was kind of fun.

Brian was still trying to climb out of the hole. He felt something funny under his toes, like a log turning. He pushed down and suddenly something white and pointed poked out of the mud.

"Look!" shouted Penny. "It's a bone." Brian couldn't believe it. Penny was right for once. It looked like a giant curved bone.

Their parents stared into the sinkhole. "Amazing," said Mrs. Casanova.

"It looks like a huge elephant tusk," said Mr. Casanova.

"It's an elephant burial ground," shouted Penny. "And I found it!"

"You fell into it!" corrected Brian. With his father's help, Brian dragged himself and the bone out of the mud hole.

"Do you really think it's an elephant's tusk?" Brian asked his parents.

"I don't know," said his father. "There never have been elephants here, but that's sure what it looks like. Maybe you should take it to the science museum and let someone there check it out."

"This could be my science project," said Brian excitedly.

"Our project!" said Penny.

"It will be nobody's project," said Mrs. Casanova, "until you both take baths."

"Can I take Flea into the bath with me?" asked Penny.

Flea was licking herself all over.

Through mud-caked eyes, Flea gave Penny a dirty look.

"I think Flea can clean herself," said Mrs. Casanova.

Brian started to lift the bone to carry it into the house. It was heavy. Penny grabbed the other end. "It's mine," she reminded him.

"I think it would be nice if you could share this discovery," said Mr. Casanova.

Penny and Brian looked at each other. *Share* was not one of their favorite words.

ERAS NOT ERRORS

The next day was Saturday, and Penny and Brian decided to take their discovery to the science museum. They waited outside for the bus. "What if there's some law against taking bones on the bus?" worried Penny.

"We have bones and they let us on the bus," said Brian.

Penny slowly nodded her head. "You know, that's very brainy," she admitted.

Brian rested the bone against a bench. He ran his hand along it. It felt smooth in parts and bumpy other places. He couldn't believe it had come from his backyard. It was way bigger than he was. The pointy end curved so that it was almost pointed back at itself. "This was some big elephant," he said.

The bus came and the driver's eyes opened wide when he saw the bone. Penny picked up the curved end and Brian picked up the heavier end. They tried to get on the lower step at the same time, but the bone was too wide.

"Penny!" said Brian. "We've got to go in sideways."

"Okay," said Penny. She kept the bone in the same position but started up the stairs with a little sidestep.

"No, Pea Brain! The bone's got to go sideways."

Penny tried to turn around, but the bone got stuck in the door.

"Hurry up or I'll make you pay an extra fare for that thing." The bus driver laughed.

Brian pushed from behind and they finally got the bone on the bus. He dug into his pocket for the exact change.

"I'd like to see the fellow who lost that false tooth," said a man sitting at the front of the bus.

"It's not a false tooth, it's a scientific discovery," said Penny, trying to keep the bone upright while Brian paid for them both.

"Why are false teeth like stars?" asked the man.

"I don't know," said Penny. "Why?"

"Because they come out at night!" he cackled.

"You'd like my Uncle Mike," said Penny.

Brian finally paid the fare. He and Penny had to stand in order to balance the bone between them. When they got to the museum, it was another struggle to get the bone up the stairs.

"Hey, Casanovas," shouted Mookie, one of Brian's best friends. "What have you got there?"

"We're not sure. It's either a bone or an elephant tusk!" shouted Penny. "I found it. Brian and I are using it for our science project."

Mookie patted his briefcase. "I'm keeping my project a secret. Say, man"—he leaned in to whisper to Brian—"I didn't know you were working with your little sister."

15

Brian screwed up his mouth. "It was an accident," he whispered back. He looked as if he had swallowed something rotten.

"He thinks he's got all the brains in the family," said Penny, who had heard every word. "But he *needs* me."

"I should have left you in that sinkhole," muttered Brian.

Mookie helped them carry the bone up the rest of the steps. The museum had opened its large hall for kids to work on their projects. In the center of the rotunda several workers from the museum were standing around a display of dinosaur bones. Some bones were lying on the floor. Some were wired together. Next to the bones was a bright orange dinosaur head with very teeny teeth.

"Hey, what happened to the old dinosaur that used to be here? Wasn't it a whole new species related to Tyrannosaurus Rex?" demanded Brian. "That thing looks fake." He pointed at the orange head.

A woman who was working on the display heard him. She was wearing glasses with bright red frames, and they slipped down on her nose. She patted the brightly colored model as if it were a pet. "There are fakes . . . and then there are real fakes," she said. "This head is part of a model of what we think a *seismosaurus* would have looked like. We'll display it next to a model of its skeleton."

"Sizemo-who?" asked Penny.

"*Seismosaurus*. It was a slender, plant-eating dinosaur that may have been as long as one hundred and forty feet," said the woman.

Brian studied the new model in progress. He thought the bright-orange head didn't look like a dinosaur's. He turned to Mookie. "Remember the old guy with the huge teeth? Now that was a real dinosaur."

"I think this dinosaur is cuter," said Penny. "I like its little teeth, but they look like they could use a brushing."

"Dinosaurs are not supposed to brush their teeth," said Brian.

The woman with red glasses laughed. "Now there's a boy with a brain in his head," she said.

"That's why we call him Brian Brain," said Penny.

"I still don't think it looks like a real dinosaur," said Brian. "Not like the old one."

The woman exchanged glances with one of her helpers. "Believe me, this one is more real than the old one."

"Are they real bones?" asked Penny.

The woman shook her head. "No, dinosaur bones are very heavy. Dinosaurs had to be very muscular to be able to hold up all that bone weight. We use a light plastic to build our models. But this time we'll have signs up that tell you the truth."

"I always tell the truth," said Penny. "My mom tells me that sometimes I'm too honest for my own good."

"Come on, Penny," said Brian, a little embarrassed. "We've got to go register."

Brian filled out a registration card for himself and Penny. Many of the kids from Brian's class were already at work on their projects. Heather was arranging her fossil collection. Denise was working on a model of a mummy. Katherine

and Tyler were working together on a model of a *Pterosaur*—a flying dinosaur.

"I'm working on a dinosaur, too," said Rafael. "I'm putting in sound effects. You'll be able to hear baby dinosaurs hatching out of eggs."

"I told you dinosaurs have been done to death," whispered Brian. He was secretly glad that they had found something so unusual.

Now they just had to figure out exactly what it was.

Mr. Vickers, Brian's teacher, had come to the science museum, too. Mr. Vickers, as usual, was looking very, very neat. His pants were pressed, and he wore a tie and a jacket, even though it was Saturday. "My goodness, Brian, where did you find this?" he asked.

"Actually, Pea Brain found it," admitted Brian.

"Pea Brain?" asked Mr. Vickers.

Brian looked down at Penny, who was giving him a dirty look. "I mean Penny," said Brian. "You know, my little sister."

Mr. Vickers smiled at Penny. Penny was a

little scared of Mr. Vickers. He always looked as if he expected something to go wrong. Mr. Vickers studied the bone. "See this curve?" he asked. "I think it might be part of a tusk from a woolly mammoth."

"A woolly mammoth!" shouted Penny. "You mean like the ones that lived with the dinosaurs?"

Mr. Vickers shook his head. "I think you've got your prehistoric eras mixed up. Perhaps somebody at the museum can help you." He picked up his clipboard and started flipping through the papers. "A Mr. Boston might be able to help you. His specialty is the prehistoric mammal. You might also try Nancy Siscoe. I heard Ms. Siscoe speak once. Her real specialty is the dinosaur, but she's brilliant about all prehistoric bones. She'll help you sort out your eras."

As they walked away, Penny whispered to Brian, "We're not even in school and he's giving us a bad grade for our errors."

"Pea Brain," scoffed Brian, "he said eras, not errors."

EVEN SOMEONE YOU LIKE CAN BE A SPACE CADET

Penny and Brian carried their bone to the scientists' offices upstairs. The first office they came to was Mr. Boston's. "Wow! Neat!" said Brian. Mr. Boston's office certainly was neat. Each shelf was dedicated to a different dinosaur family and had the names neatly printed out, both the scientific name and the name in English: *Ankylosauridaie* (Fused Lizards); *Archaeopterygidae* (Ancient Wings); *Stegosauridaei* (Roof Lizards); *Troödontidae* (Wounding Teeth).

"I hope ours is a *Troödontidae*," said Penny. "I like the sound of that."

Mr. Boston was on the phone. He looked up at them. "I'm quite busy right now. What is it?" he asked, putting his hand over the receiver.

"We don't know. That's what we want to find out," said Brian.

"Are you kids here for the science fair?" Mr. Boston asked.

Penny nodded eagerly. She noticed that Mr. Boston had a candy dish full of chocolate dinosaurs and mammoths. She realized she was very hungry.

Mr. Boston sighed. "I'm tied up now. You'd better find somebody else."

"Ms. Siscoe?" asked Brian.

Mr. Boston smiled. He had a nice smile. "Yeah," he said. "She'd be good. Take your bone to her."

Ms. Siscoe's office was just a few doors down. She was the woman they had seen in the rotunda patting the model dinosaur. Her office was a mess. It was full of books and papers shoved onto bookshelves every which way. Her desk had papers on it that looked as if they dated from prehistoric times.

Behind her desk was a model of a dinosaur,

but it didn't look like any dinosaur Brian or Penny had ever seen before. It had a bright-red beak and a purple-and-green crest on its head.

"Cool," said Penny. "It looks like Barney."

Ms. Siscoe looked flustered. "Well, not exactly." She looked at the model worriedly. "At least I hope not. What can I do for you?"

"We wondered if you could tell us where our bone comes from," Brian said.

Ms. Siscoe was still studying her model of the dinosaur. "What bone?" she asked.

Brian was a little worried. They were carrying a very large bone. If she had to ask "what bone," they were in trouble.

"This bone," said Brian, pointing to the bone.

"Just one minute," she said. "I need to find my glasses to look at it closely."

She shuffled papers around on her desk. She didn't find her glasses, but she did find a salami sandwich.

Penny giggled.

"Do you want a bite?" Ms. Siscoe asked.

"Your glasses are on your head," Penny told her.

"Oh," said Ms. Siscoe, putting them on her face. Penny noticed that the bright-red earpiece was held together with a safety pin. Ms. Siscoe pushed her glasses up on her nose. She picked up her mug to drink and spilled some coffee on a dish full of chocolate candies just like the ones in Mr. Boston's office.

"Have one," she said, taking one herself. "They taste a little like mocha. The coffee improves the taste. I'll have to suggest this to our director. These candies are one of his favorite projects."

Penny took a bite. Brian didn't want any. He wanted some answers. Ms. Siscoe picked up her coffee cup and walked around her desk to examine Penny and Brian's discovery.

"We thought it might be an elephant tusk," said Brian. "But my teacher said that it could be from a mammoth."

Ms. Siscoe stroked the curve of the bone. "This curve definitely looks like it could be from a mammoth. We had hundreds and thousands of mammoths in this area, all over North America really." She went to her bookshelf and pulled out a book by Aliki. She showed Brian and Penny a picture of a woolly mammoth.

"He's cute," said Penny. "He's got red hair like me."

"Most of the American mammoths had reddish-brown hair," said Ms. Siscoe. "Color is one of my specialties. Until recently we've made the dinosaurs and all prehistoric animals look too dull. All the big animals today—rhinos,

hippos, and elephants—are gray or brown. But they are also color-blind. Color-blind animals are often gray or brown because bright colors don't help them attract mates. But when animals can see colors, they are attracted to bright colors. They look more like birds. I've been studying dinosaur eye sockets. I believe many prehistoric animals did see color." She went to pick up her coffee cup and instead tried to drink from the horn of a rhinoceros. Brian helped her find her coffee cup, which she had left on the bookshelf.

"Can you tell us more about mammoths?" asked Brian. He found all this talk about color very interesting, but it wasn't exactly helping them with their project.

"Of course," said Ms. Siscoe. Just then the phone rang. Ms. Siscoe looked around her office, a little panicked. She couldn't find the phone.

"I hate portable phones," she muttered. She tried to follow the sound of the ringing phone.

"I think that pile of bones is ringing," said Penny. She pointed to a bunch of bones that were lying on Ms. Siscoe's couch. Penny found the phone. It was the same color as most of the bones. She handed it to Ms. Siscoe.

"Nancy Siscoe," she said into the receiver. She listened for several minutes. She played with her glasses, putting them back on top of her head. Penny wondered how soon it would be before she thought they were lost again. Finally Ms. Siscoe interrupted the person on the phone. "There is no mystery," she said. "I know what happened. I'll show you the proof."

She hung up the phone. Ms. Siscoe looked at Brian and Penny as if she had never seen them before. "We're very good at solving mysteries," said Penny.

Ms. Siscoe ran her hands through her hair, knocking her glasses into the pile of bones on her couch. "This isn't a mystery for kids," she said. "Now where were we?"

"You were going to tell us more about mammoths," said Brian.

Ms. Siscoe bit her lip. She looked as if she was very worried. "Mammoths are much younger than dinosaurs, of course. Dinosaurs lived about 165 million to 230 million years ago. Mammoths didn't appear until about 23 or 25 million years ago. Mere babies in my world."

"Like kindergartners," said Brian.

Ms. Siscoe nodded. She didn't seem to get the joke.

"Did our tusk come from a baby mammoth?" asked Penny, sounding worried.

"This is probably just a piece of the tusk," said Ms. Siscoe.

Just then Mr. Boston barged into Ms. Siscoe's office. "I have to know what's going on!" he shouted.

Penny and Brian looked guilty. They wondered what they had done wrong.

Ms. Siscoe looked even more flustered than before. "Excuse me," she said to Penny and Brian. "You two can get any information you need from the museum's computer on the main floor. There should be quite a bit on mammoths."

"This time you have gone too far," shouted Mr. Boston. Ms. Siscoe backed away from

30

him. Mr. Boston began pacing around Ms. Siscoe's office.

"Come on, Penny," whispered Brian. "We'd better go."

Penny didn't want to leave, but Brian made her pick up their tusk. He hustled Penny and the tusk out of the office.

"I wonder what Ms. Siscoe did wrong?" Penny asked.

"She probably lost an important bone," said Brian.

"Maybe we should help her," said Penny. "She kind of loses things."

"What a space cadet," said Brian.

"I thought she was brilliant," said Penny. "And I liked her."

"You can still like somebody, even if they're a space cadet," said Brian.

Penny pondered that. "You know, Brian," she said, "that's actually a smart thing to say."

Brian stared at her. It was the second time in one day that Penny had told him that he was brainy. This was getting scary.

A FUR COAT
WITH POCKETS

On Monday after school Penny and Brian went back to the museum to work on their project. Brian sat at the computer in the museum and typed in "Mammoth." Lots of cross-references came up.

"Hey, look at this," he said. "Early humans hunted mammoths and worshipped them. Some of the earliest musical instruments were made out of mammoth bones and tusks."

"Maybe I can learn to play the tusk," said Penny. "I'm musical."

Brian didn't even bother answering her. He kept reading the computer screen. "Mammoths had little tails like goats, and big shaggy coats, and amazing trunks. They weren't quite as big as elephants, but their tusks were awesome.

Some tusks were more than fifteen feet long. Prehistoric people used to make houses with mammoth tusks. They made tents using mammoth bones for poles."

"I'd like to live in a tusk tent," said Penny.

"I wish you did," said Brian.

"We could make a woolly mammoth tent out of papier-mâché and our tusk," said Penny. "I'll dress up like a cave girl."

Brian groaned.

Penny put her hands on her hips. "What's wrong with my idea?" she demanded.

Brian thought about it for a moment. Even though they had found a tusk, the museum was full of woolly mammoth tusks, and there were lots of models of woolly mammoths. But a woolly mammoth tusk tent would be different. They could show how early people had depended on woolly mammoths. Penny had actually come up with a good idea.

"Well?" demanded Penny, her hands still on her hips. "What's wrong with my idea?"

"Nothing," admitted Brian. "I just wish I had thought of it. It's pretty good. I've

never seen a tusk tent."

Just then a boy came up to them. He was pulling a red wagon that was full of little plants. "Will you be on the computer long?" he asked. "I need it, too."

"What's your project?" asked Penny. "Ours is on the woolly mammoth. They lived in the Ice Age."

"Mine is very complicated," said the boy. He clearly didn't think Penny would understand it.

"What is it?" repeated Penny. She didn't like him saying that it was something she might not understand.

"It is based on Gregor Mendel's work. You probably haven't heard of him. He worked with peas. I'm repeating his experiment. He cross-bred many types of pea plants. He was the father of modern genetics, searching for the perfect pea."

Penny grinned. "That's me."

"Maybe you can use Pea Brain here in your project," said Brian. He printed out the article on the woolly mammoth that he needed, then handed the keyboard over to the boy.

"Thanks," said the boy. "My name's George. Is her name really Pea Brain?"

"No," said Penny.

"Yes," said Brian at the same time. "Maybe you can cross her with one of your plants and see what you get. It would have to be an improvement."

"That's not funny," said Penny. "But I've got a good one. What do you get when you cross Jack Frost with Dracula?" Brian and George both shrugged.

"Frostbite!" shouted Penny. Brian and George didn't laugh.

Ms. Siscoe came by. She asked Brian and Penny how their project was going. "Great," said Penny. "We're making a mammoth-tusk tent for Pea Sprout and me."

"Who is Pea Sprout?" asked Ms. Siscoe.

"Our mammoth," said Penny.

George started giggling.

Brian covered his eyes. "Not in a million mammoth years are we calling our mammoth that."

"I found the tusk," said Penny. "I get to name it."

"Excuse me," interrupted a guard from the museum. "Ms. Siscoe, the executive director wants to talk to you right now. He wants to know what you'll say to the press about the . . ." The guard realized Penny, Brian, and George were listening. "The, uh . . . you know . . ."

Ms. Siscoe bit her lip. She looked nervous.

"Is everything all right?" asked Penny.

Ms. Siscoe tried to smile, but Penny thought she looked close to tears.

Katherine and Tyler came by dressed as *Pterosaurs*. They had stretched old stockings over some sticks to make wings.

Ms. Siscoe looked around at all the kids working on their science projects. She sighed. "It started like this for me, too," she said, more to herself than to Penny.

"I just loved science." She rubbed the back of her neck and pulled herself together. "I still do love science," she said. She went off with the guard.

Penny grabbed Brian's arm. "She's in

trouble. We should help her. Maybe somebody got sick from eating chocolates that she soaked in spilled coffee. Although I thought they were delicious."

"Penny, stop," insisted Brian. "It's none of our business. Come on, we've got a lot of work to do. Everybody else is almost finished."

Penny scowled and stamped her foot. But she knew Brian was right. Everybody else was much further along on their projects. "Okay," she relented.

Brian put her to work tearing strips of newspaper for papier-mâché. He drew a map showing how the mammoths had crossed the Bering Strait to North America. Brian drew mammoths crossing the ice floes of Alaska. He was very pleased with his work. It looked great.

Penny got bored ripping up paper. She picked up a crayon and started to draw little flowers all over Brian's map.

"What are you doing, Pea Brain?" shouted Brian.

"I'm drawing flowers for Pea Sprout and the other mammoths to eat," said Penny.

"Don't call our mammoth Pea Sprout," Brian said through gritted teeth.

"Didn't Ms. Siscoe say that mammoths ate vegetables?"

" 'They used their great tusks as shovels to scrape snow from their food,' " quoted Brian from the article he had gotten. " 'They ate grasses, herbs, twigs, and leaves buried beneath the frozen surface.' "

Penny pretended to shiver. "It's snug and warm in our mammoth tent, isn't it?" she asked.

"Kind of," said Brian. He looked down at his printout. "But mammoths were perfectly adapted for the cold. They had a humplike reserve of fat on their backs, and under their extremely thick skin was another layer of insulating fat."

Penny started to draw little dots around her flowers. She was beginning to think that Brian had gotten too much information from the computer. Too much information could be boring.

George came over to study their project.

"What's that?" he asked.

41

"Snow," explained Penny. "Did you know that woolly mammoths eat pea sprouts? They eat a lot because they're fat." She made chomping noises with her teeth.

George didn't seem to have much of a sense of humor. "Woolly mammoths are extinct," he said. "They had tiny brains like dinosaurs."

"That's not true," said Brian. "They had giant brains, like elephants."

"Dinosaurs did not have tiny brains," shouted Tyler, who had come over to look at Penny and Brian's project. "It's a myth that dinosaurs had tiny brains. Dinosaurs lasted 175 million years. That's much longer than humans have been around. And small dinosaurs like our *Pterosaurs* were evolving bigger and bigger brains."

"Nobody had a bigger brain than a mammoth," said Brian.

"Mammoths were mammals," said Katherine, who had come over looking for Tyler. "When dinosaurs ruled the earth, mammals could barely survive. Not one was bigger than a woodchuck."

"How much wood could a woodchuck chuck if a woodchuck could chuck wood?" chanted Penny.

Brian told her to hush up. He was worried. Katherine and Tyler knew an awful lot about dinosaurs, and George knew a lot about Gregor Mendel. But Brian and Penny had just started to learn about mammoths. He and Penny had the tusk, but they had a lot of catching up to do if they wanted to win.

Mookie came over to look at what they had done so far. He was still carrying his briefcase. "Pretty cool," he said, looking at the half-finished tusk tent.

"Aren't you going to tell us what your project is?" Brian asked.

Mookie shook his head. "Not till the fair opens," he said. "I don't want anybody stealing my idea." He studied George's plants.

"Hey, don't touch," said George. "The order I put them in is very important. It's how I cross-breed them that makes my project so brilliant."

"Do you know what you get when you cross

a kangaroo with a raccoon?" asked Penny.

"No," said George.

"A fur coat with pockets!" said Penny.

"That's very funny," said Tyler, giggling. "Too bad the judges don't give points for the funniest project."

Brian bit his lower lip. Tyler had a point. Penny was busy making jokes, but the judges weren't looking for funny. "Enough jokes," said Brian. "Let's get back to work."

Penny believed that there were never enough jokes, but she knew that Brian was worried. She and Brian worked every day after school and during the whole next weekend. When the mammoth tusk tent was finally finished, Brian and Penny placed the real mammoth bone at the entrance to the doorway. It looked terrific. Brian looked around. There were science projects on the solar system, lots of dinosaurs projects, and several on how to recycle waste, but nobody else had anything on the woolly mammoth.

YABBADABBADOO

On the morning of the science fair Brian and Penny put their costumes on to show their parents. "You look so cute," said Mr. Casanova, getting out the video camera. They were both wearing big, furry after-ski boots they had borrowed from their older cousins. Mrs. Casanova had allowed them to make clothes by cutting up an old fake-fur blanket that she had had since college.

Penny and Brian wrapped themselves up in fake fur and carried spears made out of mop handles. "We look ridiculous," said Brian, feeling embarrassed. He didn't even like getting dressed up for Halloween.

"You look adorable," said Mrs. Casanova.

"Mammoth hunters are not supposed to be adorable," said Brian. "We're cold. We worship the mighty mammoth. His tough, shaggy coat keeps us warm."

"We only wear fake fur," said Penny.

Brian sighed. "Penny, the earliest humans did not wear fake fur."

"They should have," said Penny. "I wouldn't want anybody going around wearing Pea Sprout's coat."

"Just keep your mouth shut when the judges come around," warned Brian.

"Ma! Brian told me to shut up!"

"I told you to keep your mouth shut—that's different."

"Now, Brian and Penny," said Mr. Casanova. "I've been so proud of the way you two have worked together on this project. Don't spoil it now."

Penny and Brian looked at each other. They *could* ruin their chances of winning if they fought. They didn't shake hands, but silently they decided on a truce.

The bus driver tried hard not to giggle when Brian and Penny got on the bus. Penny sat next to Brian. "We really could win, couldn't we?" Penny asked.

Brian had to smile. "Yeah," he admitted. He did believe they had a chance. "Finding that tusk was really a lucky break," he said. "Anybody could have done an exhibit on mammoths, but we have a real mammoth tusk to display."

Penny grinned at him. She didn't make any cracks about the fact that she was the one who had found the tusk. Her father was right. It had been fun working on this project with Brian. Finding the tusk *had* been lucky.

Penny and Brian rode together on the bus happily. They didn't fight. They didn't make nasty remarks to each other. Anyone who knew them would have been shocked.

When they got to the museum, Penny saw Ms. Siscoe pacing up and down in front of her dinosaur display. It was covered with a huge sheet.

"It looks like a dinosaur ghost," said Penny.

Ms. Siscoe looked worried. "We're going to unveil the new exhibit today. One of the judges for the science fair is a world expert on dinosaurs," she said. "I want everything to be perfect for him."

"I've got to say, I kind of liked the old one better," said Brian.

"Don't talk to me about the other one," said Ms. Siscoe. She patted the top of her head. "My glasses aren't there, are they?" she asked.

"Did you lose them again?" asked Penny.

Ms. Siscoe nodded. "I've been working all night." She sighed. "Oh, by the way, I saw your display. It looks great." She scratched her head. "In fact, I bumped into it last night."

Brian looked horrified.

"Don't worry, I didn't dent it," said Ms. Siscoe. "But I must have lost my glasses before then. Why else would I have bumped into it?"

Katherine and Tyler came flying by in their *Pterosaur* costumes. Tyler snickered when he

saw Penny and Brian in their fur shoes and fake-fur togas. "Yabbadabbadoo!" he shouted. "Which one of you is Fred Flintstone?"

"Neither, meathead," said Penny. "We're mammoth hunters."

"What I need is a glasses hunter," said Ms. Siscoe.

"We need to go," Brian said impatiently. He was anxious to get to their display. He hurried off without even saying good-bye to Ms. Siscoe.

Penny thought he was being rude. "If I have time before the judges come, I'll help you find your glasses," promised Penny. "I'm a good hunter."

"Thanks," said Ms. Siscoe.

Just then Penny and Ms. Siscoe heard a scream coming from the exhibit area.

"What's that?" asked Ms. Siscoe.

"It's Brian!" shouted Penny. "I'd know that scream anywhere."

HOW CAN YOU LOSE A MAMMOTH TUSK?!

Penny ran to their display. Brian was pointing to their tent. "It's missing! Somebody took our tusk!"

Penny stared. Brian was right. The mammoth tent was sagging. It was still up, but only because of the parts that were made of papier-mâché. The real mammoth tusk was missing.

"Our tusk! Somebody stole it! Somebody wanted to ruin our science project," Brian shouted.

Penny's mouth dropped open. "How could anybody take it? It was so heavy."

Just then George came by pulling his red wagon. It was empty. "Wheels!" shouted Penny.

George stared at her. "What's going on? Are you the cave girl who invented the wheel?"

"He has a wagon," Penny whispered to Brian. "George has always been worried that we were going to beat him. I bet he used his wagon to haul off our tusk somewhere."

Before Brian could stop her, Penny stood in front of George's wagon like a traffic cop.

"Out of way, Pea Brain," said George. "I've got to water my plants."

"You took our tusk and you've got to give it back," demanded Penny. She put her foot on the wagon so that George couldn't move it.

George tugged on it. Penny lost her balance. She tripped and went flying into George's plants, tumbling six of them to the floor.

Only a little bit of dirt came out of the pots. Penny started to pick them up.

George started shrieking. "Pea Brain—you jerk! You're messing up my whole experiment. You can't cross a tall pea plant with a fat one."

"Stop calling her Pea Brain," Brian said indignantly. "Only I call her that. And where *were* you going with that wagon?"

"What's it to you?"

"Somebody stole our tusk," said Brian. "And Penny doesn't have such a tiny brain after all. Whoever stole our tusk would have needed a wagon to move it. You're the only one with wheels here that I can see."

Just then Tyler and Katherine flew by again in their *Pterosaur* costumes. "Hey," said Penny. "Maybe they flew off with it."

George laughed. "And you said she doesn't have a pea brain." He began to fuss over his pots, scraping the dirt back into them. "Why would Katherine and Tyler want your mammoth bone? Dinosaurs didn't have anything to do with mammoths. Boy, are you mixed up."

Mookie came by. He was dressed in a houndstooth-check hat and he was carrying a magnifying glass.

"Are you supposed to be a scientist in a weird hat?" asked Brian.

Mookie shook his head. "No, I'm in costume to go with my project," he said proudly.

"So what is this mysterious project?" asked Brian. "You don't have to worry about us anymore. Our project is ruined. Somebody stole our tusk."

"You're kidding!" said Mookie. "This is a case for Inspector Mookie."

"Inspector Mookie?" demanded Penny.

"Yeah," said Mookie. He opened his brief-case. "My project is a fingerprinting kit. I made it myself. I've got a fine powder that picks up the oil from fingerprints that people leave on things. And I've got an inkpad and paper to take people's prints myself."

"Wait a minute," said Penny. "Brian and I are usually the detectives."

"And I usually help you," said Mookie. "Well, this time I'm the one who gets to solve the mystery."

"Will you help us, then?" asked Brian. "We could really use some help."

"Sure," said Mookie. "First, I've got to take your fingerprints so that we don't get them mixed up." He brought out an inkpad and rolled Penny's fingers in the ink. He pressed her fingers onto a blank sheet of paper. Then he gave her a Wash'n Dri to clean off the ink.

He did the same for Brian.

Brian wiped his hands off cleanly. But Penny still had ink on hers. She got ink smudges all over the tusk tent.

"Penny!" shrieked Brian. "Will you look at what you're doing! Just sit down and stay out of the way."

Penny sank down on the floor of their tusk tent. She bit her lip to stop herself from crying. Just a little while ago she and Brian had been feeling so good about each other. Now their

tusk had been stolen, and Brian was acting like the know-it-all brat again.

Mookie started dusting the tusk tent for prints, but he looked worried.

"What's wrong?" Brian demanded.

"I'm not finding any prints at all," he said. He shook out some more powder.

"You're making a mess," complained Brian.

"Give me a minute," said Mookie. "I'm getting one. I'm getting one." The swirls of a fingerprint came into view. He checked it against the records he had made of Penny's and Brian's prints.

"Well?" demanded Brian.

"It's not one of yours," Mookie said triumphantly.

"You've got the culprit," Penny said happily, starting to get up.

"Not by a long shot," said Brian. "Mookie, we can't fingerprint everybody."

"Wait a minute, wait a minute," said Penny. "I can get the most likely one." She took a piece of paper from Mookie's kit. She was back in business again. She scampered over to George.

"What do you want, Pea Brain?" he muttered. He was adding more dirt to his pea-plant pots.

"I wanted to say I'm sorry," said Penny. George wouldn't look at her. "I mean it," she said. "Your project is really neat. I want to tell my kindergarten teacher about your pea plants." Penny tried to make herself look as cute as possible. "Would you write down the name of that guy again—Igor?"

"Gregor," corrected George. He put down a plant and picked up the piece of paper. His hands were covered with dirt. He wrote GREGOR MENDEL in block letters.

"Your teacher will be impressed that you know his name," he said.

"Oh, thank you," gushed Penny, giving George one of her best smiles. She practically curtsied. Then she took the paper back to Mookie and Brian.

"Am I a giant brain or what?" she said, handing the paper to them. "I've got George's

fingerprints in dirt on this paper. I'm sure one will match."

Mookie took the piece of paper. He held up his magnifying glass and compared the prints to the one he had found on the tusk tent.

"No way," he said.

"No way?" wailed Penny. She thought she'd been such a good detective. She collapsed in a heap in the doorway of the tusk tent.

Just then one of the judges came by. "Isn't that sweet? You must be a little Eskimo girl in an igloo. But I'm afraid you should have done a little more research. Eskimos would never dress like that."

"It's not an igloo," Brian said through gritted teeth. "It's a mammoth-tusk tent. You see, we discovered a mammoth tusk. Prehistoric people sometimes made houses and tents out of these tusks because during the Ice Age there wasn't much else to build with."

The judges moved on to study George's plants. George explained how he had crossed pea plants in the same way that Gregor Mendel had and he hoped to create the perfect pea.

Penny scowled. "I feel like the worst pea," she said. Brian sat next to her.

"It's not your fault," he said. "I'm sorry I got so mad at you. I'm really just mad at the person who stole our tusk."

Penny felt like crying. When she felt like crying, all she wanted to do was roll over on her stomach. Sometimes when she was really mad, she kicked her feet. Brian knew all the signs. Penny rolled over on her stomach and started to kick her feet.

"Hey, stop," said Brian.

Penny was so mad that she slammed her hand on the floor. "Ouch!" she said.

She picked up a pair of bright-red glasses that had been covered up by the edge of the tent. Penny had slammed her hand down so hard that the earpieces were all bent, though one was still connected by a safety pin. "Ms. Siscoe's glasses!" exclaimed Penny. "What are they doing in our tusk tent? What was *she* doing in our tusk tent?"

"Penny, you solved the mystery," said Brian excitedly. "I bet we've even got her fingerprint. She won't get away with it."

"Not her?" gasped Penny.

"Yes, her," said Brian.

He jumped out of the tusk tent and ran down to the center rotunda, where the dinosaur was displayed.

Penny followed him. She was all mixed up. She was glad that Brian thought she had solved the mystery, but she couldn't really believe that Ms. Siscoe was the one who had stolen their tusk.

I'LL NEVER CALL
YOU PEA BRAIN
AGAIN

Brian couldn't find Ms. Siscoe anywhere. Mr. Boston stood off to the side in the rotunda talking to some reporters.

Penny and Brian could hear him saying, "I'm afraid that I didn't have anything to do with this model. This particular model was all Nancy Siscoe's project. Her little baby. She's going to unveil it."

Ms. Siscoe came out with the head of the museum and the judges. She went to the microphone. She almost bumped into it. "I am so proud to be here," she said. "First, I want to welcome all of the young people who have entered our annual science fair. You are the scientists of the future. It is your curiosity and honest enthusiasm that we will need in the twenty-first century." Ms. Siscoe's voice got louder when she said the word *honest*.

"Listen to her talk about honesty," muttered Brian. "She stole our tusk. She's probably going to use it in a mammoth display and claim she found it."

"Brian, I know we found her glasses, but I don't think Ms. Siscoe would do something like that."

"Will you two be quiet," warned George. "I want to hear what she has to say. Besides, you're making a bad impression on the judges."

Ms. Siscoe continued. "We are using the occasion of this science fair to celebrate a new exhibit right here in the rotunda. I feel I must say a few words about the previous exhibit. The museum has recently learned that the old exhibit was not, in fact, the stunning discovery of a new species of dinosaur, as we had originally thought. We regret to report that that dinosaur was pieced together with bones from several different eras. The museum is still investigating how this unfortunate error could have been made."

"Now that was a real error," whispered Brian to Penny.

"Shh," said Penny. She felt sorry for Ms. Siscoe.

"We know that many of you loved that old dinosaur," continued Ms. Siscoe, "but I think you'll all find our new exhibit equally exciting. Scientists have been making great strides in the study of what dinosaurs may have really looked like. This display reflects the new theories of dinosaur coloration. And now, if Mr. Clores, the executive director of the museum, will do the honors, we give you— *seismosaurus!*"

The executive director pushed a button and a hook on the ceiling lifted the covering off a model of a brightly colored dinosaur standing next to its skeleton. Their necks reached almost to the ceiling of the two-story rotunda.

"Oh!" breathed the crowd as one. Nobody had ever seen a dinosaur that was bright green and yellow and orange.

Penny stared at the skeleton's long middle toe. She inched her way up closer. The middle toe of the dinosaur's right foot was kind of stubby. But the middle toe on its left foot was huge!

Penny put her hand to her mouth.

"Brian," she whispered. She tugged on his arm.

"What?" asked Brian. He was looking up at the dinosaur.

"What do you get when you cross a dinosaur with a mammoth?"

"Nothing," said Brian. "You can't cross them. They lived at different times."

"I know," said Penny. "But look at the dinosaur's toe." The left toe of the dinosaur did indeed look very familiar.

Brian inched forward. "You're right. Penny, you did it again. I may never call you Pea Brain again. Ms. Siscoe is a fake scientist, and we're going to show the world. We'll do it right here in front of everybody."

Penny held back. She was so torn. Talk about mixed-up feelings! Brian had actually

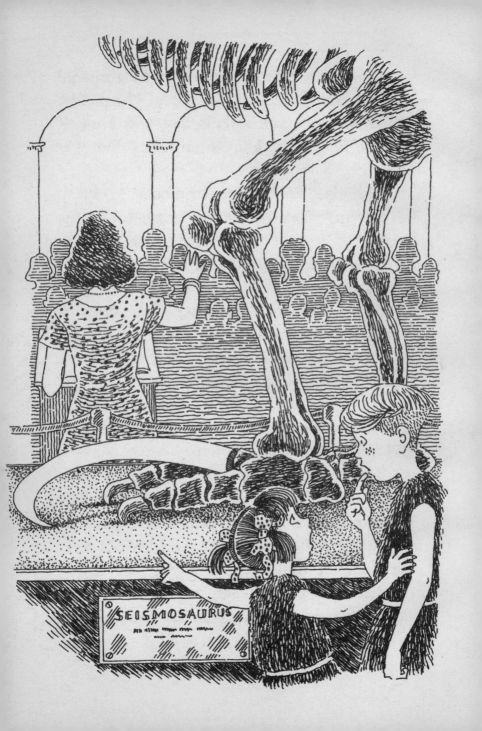

told her to her face that she wasn't a pea brain. He had said that he might never call her Pea Brain again. But Penny wasn't happy. She liked Ms. Siscoe and couldn't believe that she would mix their mammoth up with a dinosaur.

Holding Penny's hand, Brian walked right up to the head of the museum and whispered in his ear. He pointed to the toe on the dinosaur's left foot. Soon all the judges and Mr. Boston and Ms. Siscoe were staring at the dinosaur's foot.

Ms. Siscoe looked the most upset. "What is it? What is it?" she kept asking. She kept patting her pockets, hoping to find her glasses. "I need to see. I need to see."

Mr. Boston cleared his throat. "I'm afraid it's curtains for old *seismosaurus*, genus *Apatosaurus*," he said. "It's perfectly clear, even to a child, that the third prehensile toe is of the genus—"

"What is he talking about?" Penny asked Brian.

"He's telling everybody that Ms. Siscoe's

dinosaur is a fake. We already knew that."
Brian sounded smug.

"But . . . but . . ." stammered Ms. Siscoe. "I didn't put anything in this display that wasn't accurate. I . . . I can't even see it. Oh, where are my glasses?" she wailed.

Penny couldn't stand it. "Here they are," she whispered. Ms. Siscoe put on her broken glasses.

"Hey," said Brian. "You shouldn't have done that. Those glasses are important evidence."

"Evidence of what?" demanded the director.

"Evidence that Ms. Siscoe stole our tusk and stuck it on her dinosaur's foot."

"Why would I do that?" asked Ms. Siscoe.

"Yeah, why?" asked Penny.

"Whose side are you on?" hissed Brian.

"Well, it seemed like a good question," said Penny. She fidgeted. She was very nervous. She really wasn't exactly sure *whose* side she was on.

The director of the museum looked bewildered. "I think we'd better all go into my office for a moment," he said. Then he stepped up to the microphone to make an announcement. "Ladies and gentlemen, boys and girls. We will be starting the judging of the science fair in just a few minutes. But you will have to excuse the delay while we just clear up a little mix-up."

Penny looked up at the giant dinosaur and said, just loud enough for the microphone to pick up and broadcast to the whole rotunda, "It's not exactly a *little* mix-up. It's more like a *mammoth* mix-up."

EINSTEIN'S
LITTLE SISTER

The director hustled Ms. Siscoe, Mr. Boston, Penny, and Brian toward his office.

Mookie pushed his way to the front. "I have to come, too," he said.

"I think we have far too many children involved as it is," said the director.

"But I've got the fingerprint," said Mookie indignantly.

"That's right. He does," said Brian.

The director sighed. "All right," he said.

In the middle of his office was a giant carved canoe. "From Micronesia," explained the director. He sank into his desk chair. He gestured to a pot of coffee and a dish of the

museum's chocolate mammoths and dinosaurs. "Help yourselves to some coffee and chocolate if you want," he said.

Ms. Siscoe shook her head. She looked like she couldn't eat even if she had wanted to. "Mr. Clores," she pleaded. "You have to believe me. I had nothing to do with that tusk showing up on my dinosaur's foot."

"Well," said Mr. Boston, "nobody can suspect me." He took a chocolate mammoth from the dish, but he didn't eat it. "Nancy wouldn't let me near her precious project."

"This is so embarrassing," said the director. "To have our museum be connected with two fakes. And for it to come out just when everyone was here for the science fair."

"My dinosaur was never a fake," Mr. Boston complained. He gestured wildly with the chocolate mammoth. "It was a brilliant discovery of a totally new dinosaur. It would have made the museum famous throughout the world."

"It was not a brilliant discovery!" shouted back Ms. Siscoe. "I have the carbon-dated material that proves it was a total fake. A hoax designed to make him famous, not the museum."

"Wait a minute! Wait a minute!" said Brian. "First things first. We're here because Ms. Siscoe stole our mammoth tusk and put it in her dinosaur display."

"But I didn't," protested Ms. Siscoe.

Mookie stepped forward. "Let's leave it to science, shall we?" he said. He opened his briefcase.

"What's that?" asked Mr. Clores.

"It's my project for the fair," said Mookie. "It's a fingerprinting kit." He took out the paper with the fingerprint that he had found on the tusk tent. "This fingerprint was found at the scene of the crime—the home of Penny and Brian Flintstone."

"Let's keep the jokes to a minimum, please," said the director.

"Sorry," said Mookie. "I found this fingerprint on Penny and Brian's tusk tent, and it doesn't belong to either of them."

Penny was so nervous, she began to babble.

"We're early humans. We play tunes on mammoth tusks. We can't wait to invent fake fur so we don't have to wear mammoth fur."

Brian gave her a kick to shut her up.

"Could you keep to the point?" asked Mr. Boston impatiently. He finally ate the chocolate mammoth he'd been holding, then took a sip of coffee.

Penny sat quietly on the sofa and stared at his coffee mug.

"Yes, could we please continue?" said Mr. Clores.

"Certainly," said Brian. "Mookie will take Ms. Siscoe's fingerprints. It will prove that she took our mammoth bone. She lost her glasses in our mammoth-tusk tent when she stole it."

"Nancy," said the director. "Of course, you have your rights. If you don't want to give this boy your fingerprints, you don't have to."

"I will do anything to prove my innocence," said Ms. Siscoe. "I did bump into the mammoth-tusk tent last night. Maybe that's where I lost my glasses, but I did not steal their mammoth tusk. Good gracious, the museum

76

has more mammoth tusks than we know what to do with."

Mookie rolled Ms. Siscoe's fingers across his inkpad and then had her press her prints onto a piece of paper. He and Brian carefully compared them to the one they had found.

"Well?" demanded the director.

Mookie turned the single fingerprint upside down. He shook his head at Brian. "Uh . . . Ms. Siscoe's fingerprints don't match the one I found on the tusk tent," admitted Mookie sheepishly.

Ms. Siscoe sank down on the sofa next to Penny. She sighed deeply. "I would never have ruined your display," she said softly. "I care much too much about science and kids to ever do anything like that."

Penny bit her lip. She thought about the very first day when she and Brian had brought their tusk into the museum. Ms. Siscoe had made time for them even though she was so busy. Suddenly Penny leaped from her seat and grabbed Mr. Boston's mug from his hand.

"Hey," said Mr. Boston. "You're too young to be drinking coffee."

Penny spilled the remaining few sips of coffee in Mr. Clores' chocolates.

"What the! . . ." exclaimed the director.

"They're better that way," said Penny. Ms. Siscoe had to smile.

"Young lady, what are you doing?" demanded the director.

Penny handed the mug to Mookie. "I'll bet that one of the chocolate fingerprints on this cup matches the fingerprint on our tusk tent." She was looking directly at Mr. Boston.

"Don't be ridiculous," said Mr. Boston. "What possible reason would I have for taking your tusk?"

"You're not nice to little kids, and you faked a dinosaur . . . that's two strikes against you already."

"Pea Brain," warned Brian.

"I thought you weren't going to call me that anymore," hissed Penny.

"That was before you started acting like one again."

"Well, check the fingerprint," said Penny.

Mookie and Brian studied the fingerprint. It matched.

"Nancy," said the director, "I think I owe you an apology."

Mr. Boston was very angry. "What do these kids know about science?"

"More than you," said Ms. Siscoe. "I can't believe even you would stoop this low. You were so angry with me for discovering that your new dinosaur was a fake that you were willing to do anything to make me look bad— even ruin these children's entry in the science fair."

Mr. Boston looked furious. "Nancy, you are such a klutz. I watched you bump into their tusk last night. If you hadn't been such a klutz, I would never have gotten the idea." He put his hand over his mouth. He realized that he had gotten so angry that he had actually confessed.

"Mr. Boston, you're fired," said the director. "I was going to give you a second chance. I had hoped that your fake dinosaur was merely a bad mistake. But the fact that you would ruin these fine children's exhibit out of jealousy and spite toward Nancy Siscoe—that's too much. These children have shown what can happen when scientists work together honestly."

Penny was nodding happily. "I told you we could work together, Brian. You thought you had to be like Einstein and work alone."

"Oh, Einstein didn't work alone," said Ms. Siscoe. "Almost all great scientists work better when they share their ideas and discoveries. It's usually the solitary ones who turn out to be fakes."

"I still bet Einstein didn't have a little sister," said Brian. "If he had, he would never have gotten any work done."

"Oh, he did have a sister," said Ms. Siscoe. "Einstein had a little sister named Maja. And she helped him all his life."

Penny looked triumphant. "Maja. I bet he called her My Brain."

Brian rolled his eyes.

"Come on," said Ms. Siscoe. "I'll help you get your mammoth tusk back to your exhibit."

SAY THANK YOU
PEA BRAIN

Ms. Siscoe had two workmen carry the mammoth tusk back to Penny and Brian's display. The judges were making their final study of George's pea plants.

"You see, I'm trying to create the perfect pea. Like my hero, Gregor Mendel . . ." The judges took notes on George's project.

"Don't you think I am the perfect pea?" boasted Penny to Brian and Mookie. "After all, without my quick thinking, Mr. Boston would have gotten away with it."

"It was my fingerprint kit that saved the day," said Mookie.

Brian wasn't paying attention to either of

them. He was watching the judges with George. "Come on Penny," he said, grabbing her by the fur. "The judges are about to come to our exhibit next. It's the last time they'll look at it."

"And right after they see you, the judges will be over to my aisle," said Mookie. "I've got to display my fingerprints." Mookie hurried off.

Brian could see that the judges were on their way. He tried to make sure that the tusk was in exactly the right position. Then he tried to make Penny stand up straight. The judges walked around the mammoth-tusk tent.

"This is a genuine mammoth tusk at the entrance," explained Brian.

"The mammoth's name was Pea Sprout," chirped in Penny.

Brian gave her a dirty look.

"How cute!" said one of the judges.

Penny grinned.

"May we look inside?" asked one of the judges. Brian then took the judges through their whole exhibit. He showed them how he

and Penny had tried to display how early people had needed mammoths.

"Just like brothers need sisters," added Penny. "Even Einstein." She poked Brian in the ribs. Brian tried hard not to poke her back.

The judges went on to the aisle where Mookie's exhibit was.

"Do you think we won?" Penny asked.

"Pea Sprout!" sputtered Brian. "Our mammoth's name isn't Pea Sprout!"

"Then what is it?" Penny asked.

Brian stared at the tusk. The truth was that he had started to think of their mammoth as Pea Sprout.

"Pea Sprout!" said Penny, triumphantly stroking the tusk.

Just then Mookie came by. "Did the judges look at your fingerprints?" Brian asked.

"Yeah," said Mookie. "They took notes—but I couldn't tell if they liked it. How did you do?"

"We don't know," said Brian. "I'm nervous."

"Let's go to the center of the rotunda," said Mookie. "That's where they're going to make the announcement."

Mookie and Brian and Penny made their way through the crowd. Tyler and Katherine still had on their flying dinosaur costumes. George was in the front, biting his nails.

"What's happening?" asked Penny. She was too short to see over all the taller kids.

"The judges are whispering to Mr. Clores and Ms. Siscoe," said Katherine.

"They're taking a long time," complained George.

"I can't stand the suspense," said Mookie.

"You're a detective," said Penny. "You're supposed to like it."

Brian laughed. "She's right," he said.

Penny grinned. Brian had laughed at her joke. She loved it when Brian laughed with her—not at her—that was almost as good as winning.

Finally, somebody tapped the microphone.

"Would Penny and Brian Casanova come forward along with Mookie Lowry."

"Do you think we're in trouble?" asked Penny. "Maybe they're mad at us for proving that Mr. Boston stole our tusk."

Brian took Penny's hand.

The director of the museum helped Penny onto the podium.

"For the first time in the history of our science fair we have a tie for first place," Mr. Clores announced. "Mookie Lowry's entry is a very ingenious (and, as it turned out, useful) fingerprinting kit. He wins first place in a tie with Penny and Brian Casanova for their exhibit featuring a real mammoth tusk and how early humans might have used it."

Ms. Siscoe led the applause. Penny waved her hands over her head like a prizefighter. She stepped forward to the microphone. "It all started on a rainy day . . ." she began.

Brian pulled her away from the microphone. "Just say thank you, Pea Brain," he muttered.

"Thank you, Pea Brian," said Penny.

Everybody in the whole rotunda laughed. Even George, who won fourth place.

Don't miss these other adventures
Starring Brian and Pea Brain
by Elizabeth Levy

School Spirit Sabotage

School Spirit Week is supposed to be fun, but it's turned into a whodunit! There's a prankster on the prowl and Brian Brain, detective extraordinaire, has his work cut out for him. Can Brian think up a prankster-catching plan in time to save the day?

Rude Rowdy Rumors

Klutzy Brian is surprised when he actually makes the soccer team, but he's shocked when someone starts spreading rumors about him. He doesn't know where to turn to catch the culprit. Can Brian's pea brain sister Penny save her brother's reputation?